Porcupine's Pajama Party

Terry Webb Harshman

Pictures by
Doug Cushman

HarperTrophy®
A Division of HarperCollins*Publishers*

To Anna Lee and Harrison, with love
T.W.H.

For Kim the Owl
D.C.

HarperCollins®, ☕®, Harper Trophy®, and I Can Read Book®
are trademarks of HarperCollins Publishers Inc.

Library of Congress Cataloging-in-Publication Data
Harshman, Terry Webb.
    Porcupine's pajama party.

    (An I can read book)
    Summary: Porcupine bakes cookies, watches a
monster movie, and gets scared in the dark when
his two best friends sleep over.
    [1. Porcupines—Fiction. 2. Fear—Fiction.
3. Night—Fiction] I. Cushman, Doug, ill.
II. Title. III. Series.
PZ7.H25625Po 1988   [E]   87-45681
ISBN 0-06-022248-4
ISBN 0-06-022249-2 (lib. bdg.)
ISBN 0-06-444140-7 (pbk.)

First Harper Trophy edition, 1990.

Contents

The Invitations

Porcupine was eating lunch.

He put peanut butter

on celery sticks.

"I love peanut butter boats

with honey sandwiches,"

he said.

"There is only one thing wrong.

I am lonely."

Suddenly,

Porcupine had a wonderful idea.

"I will invite Otter and Owl

to a pajama party."

He wrote a note to Otter

and a note to Owl.

The notes said,

"I am having a pajama party tonight.

Let me know if you can come.

Porcupine."

6

Porcupine hurried to Otter's house.

He put the note in Otter's mailbox.

He ran over the hill

to Owl's tree.

He dropped the note

through Owl's letter slot.

Then Porcupine hurried home.

He fixed a cup

of peppermint tea.

"They will be calling any minute.

I will sip my tea

while I wait."

Porcupine sipped his tea

and waited.

He stared at the telephone.

"My cup is empty

and nobody has called.

Maybe Otter did not look

in his mailbox.

Maybe Owl is away this weekend."

Porcupine was getting worried.

Suddenly,

the telephone rang.

"This is Owl,"

said a voice.

"Owl who?" asked Porcupine.

"The owl that you invited

to a pajama party," said Owl.

"Oh," giggled Porcupine,

"*that* Owl.

Please come.

Otter is invited too."

10

"I would love to come,"

said Owl, "except . . ."

"Except what?" asked Porcupine.

"I want to watch a scary movie

on television tonight,"

said Owl.

"We can watch it here,"
said Porcupine.
"It will be more fun
getting scared together."
Owl thought
about being alone and scared.
"I will be happy to come
to your pajama party,"
he said.

"What is the name of the movie?"

asked Porcupine.

"*Monster Bat*," said Owl.

Porcupine shivered.

"Come before it gets dark," he said.

"I will," said Owl.

"Good-bye."

13

The phone rang again.

It was Otter.

"I want to come to your pajama party,"

said Otter, "but . . ."

"But what?" asked Porcupine.

"I am trying a new cookie recipe tonight,"

said Otter.

"We can bake your cookies here,"

said Porcupine.

"Owl is coming too."

15

"Goody," said Otter.

"I will be there!"

"Cross your toes?"

asked Porcupine.

"And squeeze my nose,"

promised Otter.

"Come before dark,"

said Porcupine.

"Okay," said Otter.

"See you later."

Baking Cookies

Otter opened his recipe box
and pulled out a card.
"This recipe has been handed down
from otter to otter,"
he said.
"So it *must* be yummy!"

"I will measure the flour,"
said Porcupine.

"I will open the chocolate bits,"
said Owl.

"And *I* will stir,"
said Otter.

They mixed everything together.

"Let's sample the dough,"

said Owl.

Everyone took a big bite.

"We forgot the vanilla,"

said Otter.

He stirred some in.

They gobbled more of the dough.

"Much tastier," said Porcupine.

"Quite good," said Owl.

Otter pulled a small bottle

out of his pocket.

"What is that?" asked Porcupine.

"The Otter family secret,"

Otter said proudly.

"I bet it is powdered fish tails,"

said Owl.

Otter added a pinch of the powder.

He stirred and tasted.

"Mmmm, perfect!"

Owl tried some.

"Delicious!" he said.

21

Porcupine sniffed the bowl.

He thought

about powdered fish tails.

"Afraid?" teased Owl.

Porcupine took a bite.

"Stupendous!" he shouted.

They tasted and sampled.

They nibbled and gobbled.

Porcupine got a cookie sheet.

"I will do the first row,"

said Otter.

He plopped down three cookies.

It was Porcupine's turn.

He dug the spoon into the bowl.

He scraped and scraped.

"My spoon is empty,"

he said.

"You did not dig deep enough,"

said Owl.

Porcupine dug to the bottom
of the bowl.

There was a hollow,
clickety-clack sound.

"The dough is gone!"

shouted Owl.

"POOEY!" cried Otter.

"I do not want a recipe
that only makes *three* cookies!"

25

He threw the recipe into the trash.

Porcupine rubbed his tummy.

"I am not really in the mood

for cookies," he said.

"I guess one is enough

for me," said Otter.

"Me too," agreed Owl.

"I am on a diet."

Porcupine popped the cookies

into the oven.

Monster Bat

It was time for the movie.

Monster Bat flew

into the sheriff's bedroom.

Slowly, he crept

to the sheriff's bed.

His mouth opened wide

and showed long, pointed teeth.

He was ready to bite!

"Guess what?" blurted Otter.

Owl jumped.

Porcupine screamed.

"What is it?" snapped Owl.

"I think I have to go
to the bathroom," said Otter.

"What do you mean, you *think*?"
said Owl.

"Don't you know for sure?"

"Yes," said Otter.

"I know for sure

that I have to go.

Does anyone else?"

"Not me," said Porcupine.

"Me neither," said Owl.

Otter lowered his head.

"I think I am afraid

to go by myself.

Monsters get you

when you are alone."

"There you go *thinking* again,"
said Owl.

"Besides,

monsters are not real."

"Don't worry," said Porcupine.

"I will go with you."

Owl heard them run down the hall.

Then

he could not hear anything.

He was alone.

"What is taking them so long?"

wondered Owl.

"I do not like being alone."

Outside,

a frog croaked.

The wind howled.

"WAIT FOR ME!" shouted Owl.
"MONSTERS GET YOU
WHEN YOU ARE ALONE!"

He ran to the bathroom.

"Hurry up, you guys!

You don't want to miss the movie."

"We don't?" asked Otter.

"No, you don't," said Owl.

They watched the rest of the movie.

Then it was time for bed.

"Can I sleep in the middle?"

asked Otter.

"I am the youngest."

"I should sleep in the middle,"

said Owl.

"I am the smallest."

"Those are good reasons,"

said Porcupine.

"But I will sleep in the middle."

41

"You are not the youngest,"
said Otter.

"Or the smallest," said Owl.

42

"No," said Porcupine,

"but I have *three* good reasons.

It is *my* house,

my pajama party,

and *my* bed."

"Those are good reasons,"

agreed Otter and Owl.

Everyone climbed into bed.

The Scariest Thing

"Porcupine," said Otter,

"what is the scariest thing

you can think of?"

"A big, hairy beast

that eats porcupines,"

said Porcupine.

"Sometimes I see it in my closet."

Otter looked at Owl.

"Owl," he said,

"what is the scariest thing

you can think of?"

"A giant, black creature

that eats owls," said Owl.

"Sometimes it taps on my window."

Porcupine and Owl looked at Otter.

"What is *your* scariest thing?"

they asked.

"A slithery, green monster
that eats otters,"
he replied.
"Sometimes I hear it
under my bed."

The room looked very spooky.

Suddenly,

Porcupine screamed.

"OTTER! OWL! HELP!

The beast that eats porcupines

is in my closet!"

Owl turned on the light.

He went to the closet

and picked something up.

"Look, Porcupine," he said.

"Your hairy old beast

is just some hairy old blankets!"

Porcupine sat up.

"Blankets sure can look mean

in the dark," he said.

Owl turned off the light

and got into bed.

Suddenly,

he heard something.

TAP…SCREEEEEEEE…TAP-TAP…

"OTTER! PORCUPINE! SAVE ME!"

he cried.

"The creature that eats owls

is at the window!

It has glowing eyes!"

Otter ran to the window.

"Don't worry, Owl.

It is only a branch

scraping against the glass.

The glowing eyes you saw

are only fireflies."

Owl looked at the window.

"Fireflies look like monster eyes
in the dark," he said.

Otter climbed into bed.

Everything was quiet.

And then,

"PORCUPINE! OWL! HELP ME!"

screamed Otter.

"The slithery, green monster

is under the bed!

I hear its lips smacking!"

Porcupine flipped on the light

and looked under the bed.

"You can relax, Otter," he said.

"This monster is not slithery *or* green.

It is tiny and furry,

with big ears."

Otter peeped under the bed.

There was a little mouse

eating a crust of bread.

"This mouse sounds like a *moose*
in the dark," said Otter.

Everyone burst out laughing.

They felt very silly.

Porcupine turned off the light.

"Imagine being afraid of blankets,"

he laughed.

"Or little fireflies," hooted Owl.

"Or," giggled Otter,

"munching mouse lips!"

They laughed even harder.

Otter, Owl, and Porcupine

were no longer afraid.

They were warm and safe and happy.

They snuggled together

and drifted off to sleep.